This Bing book belongs to:

....

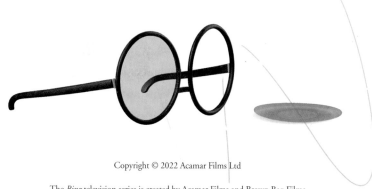

The *Bing* television series is created by Acamar Films and Brown Bag Films
and adapted from the original books by Ted Dewan.

Bing's New Friend is based on the original story 'Nicky' written by Mikael Shields and Claire Jennings. *Bing's New Friend* was first
published in Great Britain by HarperCollins *Children's Books* in 2022 and was adapted from the original story by Rebecca Gerlings.

HarperCollins *Children's Books* is a division of HarperCollins*Publishers* Ltd
1 London Bridge Street, London SE1 9GF

www.harpercollins.co.uk

HarperCollins*Publishers*
1st Floor, Watermarque Building, Ringsend Road, Dublin 4, Ireland

1 3 5 7 9 10 8 6 4 2

ISBN: 978-0-00-849767-5

Printed in Italy

MIX
Paper from
responsible sources
FSC C007454

FSC
www.fsc.org

This book is produced from independently certified FSC™ paper
to ensure responsible forest management.

For more information visit: www.harpercollins.co.uk/green

Bing's New Friend

HarperCollins *Children's Books*

Round the corner, not far away,
Bing is visiting **Sula** today.

"You are **vooooshing,** Hoppity!" says Bing.

Bing is really looking forward to seeing Sula!
They're going to make rippy pictures together.

When they arrive at Sula's house, Amma opens the door and tells them that Sula has a visitor.

"Oh," says Bing. He wonders who it could be.

"Bysie-bye, Bing," says Flop. "Amma can ring me if you need me. I've just a couple of things to pick up."

"Oh. Bye, Flop," says Bing.

Bing goes inside the house.

"Hello, Bing!" says Sula excitedly.

"Erm . . . hello, Sula," replies Bing.

"This is my cousin,
Nicky," says Sula.
"Isn't he *adorable*?"

Bing has never met Nicky before and is a little unsure.
Then, he notices what's in Nicky's hand.
"Oh, that's *my* speedy car!" says Bing.

"Nicky loves it, Bing!" replies Sula.

"Car!" says Nicky. **"Brrrrm!"**

"Erm . . . yes," says Bing.

As Nicky plays
with Bing's speedy
car, Bing and
Sula make
rippy pictures.

"I'm going
to do the most
sparkliest star!"
says Sula.

"I'm going to do
Flop," Bing says.
"Erm . . . will he
be back soon?"

"Yes, Bing, he will,"
smiles Amma. "Well,
my carrot cake
won't bake itself."

On her way to the kitchen, Amma sees Nicky with the basket of blocks. He giggles as he tips it over.

CRASH!

"Careful, Nicky," laughs Amma.

"Nicky, come and do some **rippy pictures!**" Sula calls.

Nicky comes over and starts to sloooowly tear up some paper.

Riiiiipppp!

Bing sighs. He still isn't sure about Sula's cousin, Nicky.

"Brrrm! Brrrm!"

Nicky runs round the table and almost drives
the speedy car into Bing's pile of rippy paper.

"Oh, careful!" says Bing.

"Be nice to Nicky," Sula tells him. "He's only little!"

"I *am* being nice! He is playing with *my* speedy car," says Bing.

"Oh, yes," laughs Sula.

While Sula goes to look for some purple rippy [...]er,
Nicky holds up the speedy car to show B[...]

"Car **vooosh!**" he says.

"Oh . . . okay," replies Bing.

Bing takes Nicky to the slide.

"Look!" says Bing. "You can *voosh* my speedy car down the slide! I can show you. One . . . two . . . three . . .

VOOOSH!"

Then, Bing has another idea. "*You* can *voosh* down the slide too. I'll show you!"

Bing climbs to the top of the slide while Nicky watches him.
"Okay!" he says. "One . . . two . . . three . . .

VOOOSH!"

As Bing reaches the bottom,
Nicky climbs up to the top – all by himself!

"VOOOOOSH!"

Nicky shouts.

He slides all the way to the
bottom but catches his feet on
the edge of the mat. As Nicky tumbles,
his glasses fall off and a lens pops out.

"Oh no!" says Bing.

"Oh no! Nicky!"
cries Sula,
rushing to help him.
"Bing! You *should*
have looked
after Nicky!"

"I did!"
says Bing.

"What's all this shouty hoo-ha?"
asks Amma, walking over.

"Bing let Nicky go down the slide and
now his glasses are broken!" replies Sula.

"Nicky did want to go on the slide,
and you're not being fair, Sula!" says Bing.

"Well, at least Nicky's not broken," says Amma.

"I really want Flop," says Bing.

Then, Nicky holds out his glasses to show Bing.

"Bing!" says Nicky, as he takes
the lens that has fallen out . . .

. . .**CLICK!** He puts it back in again.

"Glasses!" giggles Nicky.

"Ohhh! Nicky!" says Bing.

"Bing okay. Glasses!" repeats Nicky, giving Bing a big hug.

"Oh, clever boy!" says Amma.

"Thank you, Nicky," says Bing.

"Erm . . . sorry, Bing," says Sula.

"Sorry, Sula," he replies.

"Oh! GOOD apologising!" says Amma.

"Okay . . . who's ready for my special carrot cake?" asks Amma.

"Oh, me!" everyone shouts.

DING-DONG!

It's Flop!

Bing runs to the door and hugs him tight.

"Ohhh, I missed you, Flop!"

"Hello, Bing!
I missed you too!"

"We've got
carroty cake!"
calls Bing,
running ahead.

"Come on in, Flop,"
says Amma.
"Cup of tea?"

"Oh, lovely!"
he answers.

In the kitchen, everyone eats
the delicious carroty cake.

"Yummy, Amma!" says Sula.

Bing agrees. "Mmm, cake!"

"CAKE!" says Nicky.

"Awww, Nicky!" everyone laughs.

**New friends . . . they're a Bing thing!
And a Nicky thing too!**